Buttception
A Butt Within A Butt Within A Butt

CHUCK TINGLE

Where does the miracle of science end and magic begin?

- Pounded In The Butt By My Own Butt

CONTENTS

ACKNOWLEDGMENTS

Thank you to my number one fans, you are the soul of books and you make love real. Real fans make books kiss the sky.

No thanks to Ted Cobbler, a real piece-of-work devil man.

ANALLY YOURS, THE UNICORN SAILOR

Years ago, I would have never considered myself much of a writer, but the more that you do something the better you get at it, and some days during the last few months it felt like I was writing more than I'm speaking.

It wasn't always this way, of course, and in my college days I was barely capable of fumbling my way to a passing English grade. Math was more of my thing, and the finesse that beloved authors used to string together their prose escaped me completely.

This, however, all changed on a warm summers eve, when I was strolling casually along the docks of San Francisco. The sun was just about to disappear beyond the horizon, casting the entire bay in a purple and orange glow and causing my shadow to stretch out forever like black taffy behind me. The seagulls were crying out as they fluttered around the boats of the nearby marina, seemingly mourning the slow death of their beloved fading sun. It was breathtaking.

Unfortunately, I wasn't really in the mood to enjoy it completely. Instead, my mind was haunted by visions of my girlfriend, Kortos, who was now painfully my ex-girlfriend. The break up was fresh, no older than two days, and I was far from ready to let it go.

My heart was broken, and at that point I was utterly convinced that I would never find another lover again.

That is, until I saw him.

Looking out across the marina, my gaze stopped on an incredibly handsome unicorn who was in the midst of securing his large sailboat to the dock with a thick rope. The unicorn was absolutely gorgeous, toned and muscular with broad shoulders and biceps that could crack walnuts.

All my life, I had only found myself attracted to woman, but the second that I laid my eyes on this handsome unicorn something changed deep within me. This mysterious sailor beast had a hold on my heart, and now there was no going back.

Immediately, I start to make my way down towards the water. I have never had much confidence when it comes to the approach, but this creature's beauty was so powerful, so seductive, that it feels as though *not* talking to him would be even harder to consider. This is a once in a lifetime moment, and I know that I have to strike while I have the chance; for better, or for worse.

The unicorn looks up as I make my way down the dock towards him, smiling as our eyes meet.

"Hey." I say, stopping in front of him, my heart pounding hard within my chest.

"Hi there." Says the unicorn.

I suddenly realize that I have nothing else to say, completely unprepared for the inevitable conversation that would occur after our introductions.

The awkward silence between us seems to last forever, until I finally muster up the courage to stammer out a follow up question for this majestic beast.

"Nice boat." I finally say. "What's it called?"

"The Butt." The unicorn tells me confidently. "Do you sail?"

I shake my head, "No. I mean, I've always wanted to but my girlfriend hates the ocean."

The unicorn cracks an uncomfortable smile as the word girlfriend leaves my lips, so I quickly correct myself.

"Ex-girlfriend." I say.

"Oh!" The unicorn responds in turn. "I'm so sorry to hear that."

I suddenly realize that this unicorn is just as interested in me as I am in him, and from here on out a strange calm falls over me. I'm cool, casual and collected.

"What's your name?" I ask the handsome nautical beast.

"Hunter." The unicorn says, reaching out and shaking my hand with his hoof.

The second that we touch, a sharp chill runs down my spine, a signal that something is happening here way beyond a mere chance meeting. This is special.

"I'm Tuck, it's nice to meet you. I'm sorry if this is forward." I say. "But, would you be interested in grabbing some dinner tonight?"

"Right now?" Laughs Hunter.

"Yeah." I tell him, desperately aching to avoid rejection. "There are some great restaurants along the water here. It's my treat."

Hunter looks me up and down for a moment, clearly focused on some kind of private inner debate. Finally, he nods. "Yeah, let's go."

It's not long before we are seated at a nearby restaurant that overlooks the San Francisco bay. The place is a little out of my price range, but I'm hell bent on impressing this beautiful beast tonight, and so far it seems to be working.

I've ordered a well-seasoned surf and turf, meticulously presented and piping hot on the plate before me.

Being a unicorn, Hunter has ordered a large portion of hay, which he munches on happily.

"How is it?" I ask.

"Amazing." Hunter tells me. "This is some of the best hay I've had in a long, long time. Thanks for taking me here."

I lean back in my chair and smile. "Is it weird how comfortable I feel around you? I mean, we've only just met but I feel like I've known you my entire life."

The unicorn stops chewing, renegade straws of hay dangling from his lips. "No, I feel it, too."

His admission fills my heart with warmth, an incredible sensation of mutual comfort and admiration now coursing between us. The rest of the meal slowly evolves into the best date of my life, full of lighthearted conversation and beautifully personal revelations about life and love. I explain to Hunter that I've never been with another man before, unicorn or human, and he puts my mind at ease, explaining that it's not entirely gay if a relationship is between a man and a beast. I tell him that I don't mind either way. Maybe I've always been gay and I just didn't know it until now?

As the night begins to come to a close, I finally muster up the courage to ask Hunter on a second date.

"So… this was a lot of fun." I start. "I thing you're incredible and I'd like to see you again sometime. Maybe this Friday?"

The unicorn gets strangely quiet and suddenly my heart skips a beat. I know that I've done nothing wrong, but based on Hunter's reaction there is clearly something going on here that I'm not yet fully aware of.

"What is it?" I ask.

Hunter lets out a long sigh, his gaze drifting over my shoulder and out across the vast, black waters beyond. "I knew this was going to happen."

"What was going to happen?" I question, frustrated as I reach out across the table and take his hoof in my hand. "What's wrong?"

"I can't see you on Friday. In fact, I don't know if I'll ever see you again." Hunter says.

Immediately, I find it hard to breath. I sit straight up in my chair, reeling from the unicorn's startling admission and more than a little confused. "What do you mean?" I demand to know, struggling to keep my emotions in check.

"Here's the deal." Hunter says, tears welling up in his eyes. "I'm leaving tonight, right when we get back to the docks. I'm about to start a year long journey to sail around the world in The Butt."

"Oh my god." Is all that I can say. I'm not upset with Hunter, just utterly, savagely heartbroken.

"I want you to know that I feel it too." The unicorn admits. "I feel this love between us and I know that it's as real as it gets."

I want to beg Hunter not to go, to demand that he stays with me here in San Francisco, but I just can't do it. I can already tell that the handsome unicorn is having a hard enough time as it is, and I don't want to make this any worse on him.

"I understand." I say, the words burning my soul as they escape from my lips. "Go."

"Tuck." Hunter says, a single tear streaming down his face. "I'll wait for you."

My body is flooded with emotions now, almost too much to bear. "You will?"

"Of course." Hunter says. "I've never met anyone like you before. I need to go on this trip, but when I return we can be together."

I can't help myself; I stand up right then and there, in the middle of the restaurant, and walk around the table, throwing my arms around Hunter. "I love you so much." I confess.

"I love you, too." Says my gay unicorn lover. "Mark my words… When I see you again, I'll do something that shows you just how much I love you. I promise."

When we finally finish our embrace I sit back down, wiping my eyes.

"I'm not going to have the internet or phone service." Explains the unicorn. "But I can give you a map of when and were I'll be at every port. You'll be able to send me letters that I can pick up at the local post office. Will you write to me?"

"Of course I'll write to you." I promise Hunter. "Every day."

The unicorn nods, his majestic horn glinting in the moonlight that streams through the window next to him. "Good… I guess I'll see you in a year then."

The first few days are the hardest. As Kortos moves her things out of our apartment, I patiently wait for the first letter from Hunter to arrive. We have agreed that he will start our exchange and then I will respond, leaving me with nothing to do but wait.

The days seem to stretch on forever.

It remains like this until finally, one fateful morning, I open up my mailbox to see a beautifully folded letter waiting for me.

Immediately, I take the tiny parcel inside and open it while sitting nervously at the dining room table, anxious for whatever Hunter has to say.

"Dearest Tuck." I read aloud to myself. "Never before have a felt such a longing in my heart. You are the light in my life, a brilliance that I never knew was possible until now. You cast out the darkness and replace it with a whole new world. This will be a long year, but it will be worth it, and at the end of this year I want you to give yourself to me, wholly and completely, so that I can fuck your brains out."

His words make me tremble with desire, and soon enough I find myself unzipping my jeans, my hand slipping down past the waistband of my underwear and grabbing a hold of my rock hard cock. I begin to stroke myself off as I read the rest of the unicorn's beautifully crafted letter.

"I can't wait to be inside of you." I read aloud, my voice quaking. "To shove this fat unicorn cock up your ass and make you beg for more."

Even though I have just begun reading, I suddenly find myself aching to cum, to shoot my pent up load as I recite Hunter's romantic words aloud.

"I want to blast my load all over your chiseled human face and watch you lick my unicorn seed from your lips." I read.

Immediately, I start cumming, ejecting my hot jizz onto the floor beneath the dinner table. "Fuck!" I cry out, no longer reading as I buckle forward, unable to contain the immense pleasure that explodes within me.

When the sensation finally passes I fall back into my chair, exhausted. I pick up the letter and continue to read the rest of it.

"In other news, I've decided to start collecting beach glass from every port that I stop in. I'm hoping to start an online business where I sell it to people from around the world." I recite.

I can't help but smile at Hunter's ambitious nature, and my expression grows even wider when I reach the bottom of the page.

"I love you, and I can't wait for the day that we will be together again." I read aloud. "Anally yours, Hunter."

Just below his signature, Hunter has left the pink marking of his puckered butthole, pressed against to page in a perfect starfish after applying a liberal helping of lipstick.

The letters continue back and forth like this for months, ranging from in depth personal confessions to hardcore erotic prose. Every time I open my mailbox to find one of his notes it feels like Christmas morning; with me running inside and tearing the letter open in a frantic attempt to get at whatever gay musings can be found within.

One day, however, everything changes. I open my letter and my jaw drops, blown away by the words that stare back at me from the page.

"Dearest Tuck." I read aloud. "I am writing to inform you that my beach glass business has taken off dramatically. I am now a billionaire and would like to send my private helicopter to come and pick you up in the very spot we met, at noon, so that it can carry you to the Bahamas where I will be waiting nude on the beach, ready to make love to you. Anally yours, Hunter."

Immediately, I jump up from my chair and begin to pack my things.

As our helicopter draws closer to the Bahaman beach, I strain to catch a glimpse of my unicorn lover. It has been months since we've seen each other in person, months since that incredible night when the two of us learned what love truly was.

"There's the shore!" My pilot says over his headset, pointing down at the white sand below.

It's then that I spot Hunter, laying out on the edge of the water with his massive unicorn cock completely exposed. He is ripped beyond belief and tanned to perfection after months out on the water. Immediately, tears of joy begin to fill my eyes.

The helicopter lands on the sand and before the pilot can say another word I've leapt from the craft, sprinting down the beach towards Hunter.

Meanwhile Hunter is galloping towards me, his massive rod bouncing with an impressive heft as he moves. When the two of us finally meet in the middle there is an explosion of passion, our embrace immediately morphing into a zealous whirlwind of kisses that causes the two of us to collapse into the sand.

Hunter is on top of me, his muscular body pressed hard against mine as the tide pulses below us in a cool succession of gentle waves.

"I've missed you so fucking much." I tell the powerful creature.

"You have no idea." Hunter says, kissing me deeply once more.

We roll around in the sand like this for a while until I just can't take it anymore, pushing my unicorn lover back so that he's laid out on the beach with his massive shaft pointing upward like a glorious pink rocket.

"I've been wanting to do this for a long time." I tell him with a wink, then opening wide and take Hunter's enormous dick down my throat. I push down as deep as I can and hold him there, allowing all twelve inches of his hard unicorn shaft to slip into my depths.

Hunter lets out a long, satisfied moan, clearly impressed with my skills as an oral lover and fully aware of the fact that he is the first man I have ever been with. In the months leading up to this encounter, I have been practicing my technique with a banana, and it appears to be paying off.

"Holy shit, Tuck." Hunter groans. "You are so good."

When I finally run out of air I come up with a frantic gasp, a rope of saliva hanging gracefully from my lips.

I give Hunter a wink. "You ain't seen nothing yet."

Immediately, I get back to work on the unicorn's giant rod, bobbing my head up and down across the length of his shaft. I can feel Hunter's muscular abs tense up and release, his hips moving along in unison with my expertly performed movements.

As I service Hunter with my mouth I reach up and cradle his fuzzy unicorn balls, massaging them gently while I lick him from base to tip.

"I want to fuck you." My unicorn lover eventually says. "I want to pound that tight little twink asshole."

"Please." I beg. "Please fuck me. It's all that I want."

Immediately, I turn around and place myself before Hunter in the sand on my hands and knees, tearing off my shirt and shorts and popping my bare ass back towards him.

The unicorn eyes me up, taking in my toned physique as I tempt him with my puckered gay hole.

"I need you inside of me." I admit. "I'm anally yours."

"Forever?" Hunter asks, climbing up onto his hooves and clopping into position on the wet sand behind me.

"Forever." I tell him.

Hunter places his massive unicorn rod up against the rim of my butt, teasing the edge of my tightness while I reach back with one hand and hold myself open for him. My unicorn lover pushes forward, slowly but firmly, letting me feel every aching moment of my butthole spread to accommodate his enormous size.

"Oh fuck, you are so big!" I cry out, my body flooded with a mixture of pain and pleasure as I gradually take the length of Hunter's monstrous rod. My asshole is stretched to its absolute limits, struggling to contain the thickness within.

Soon enough, Hunter has reached maxed out my asshole, his cock fully inserted within me and held firmly at the hilt. My body has just finished growing accustomed to his size when the muscular unicorn begins to pump in and out of my depths, slowly at first and then gaining speed.

I brace myself against the sand before me, the cool waves rushing in and out of my fingers as the massive cock rushes in and out of my butt. Almost immediately I can feel the strange and unfamiliar sensation of prostate orgasm blossoming within. My body is quaking hard beneath Hunter's weight, aching and trembling as a vicious cocktail of lustful emotions pulses through me.

"I'm getting close." I groan, Hunter's thrusts continuing to hammer away at my backside. "I think I'm gonna cum!"

I reach down and start to frantically beat off my hard rod, my body quaking with desire until suddenly Hunter pulls me up and stops me.

"Oh no you don't." My majestic unicorn lover says with a laugh. "I need you to blow that hot load inside of me."

I climb to my feet as the unicorn sailor motions for me to mount him from behind. I do as I'm told, climbing aboard the massive beast so that I'm clutching tightly to his waist while I hang down off of the back. My cock is perfectly positioned at the entrance of Hunter's asshole, and as the unicorn takes off galloping down the beach I push into him firmly.

Now holding on for deal life, I find myself riding Hunter along the shoreline, each and every gallop pushing me in and out of his tight asshole. The sensation is incredible, and as the cool sea breeze whips past my face I find myself overwhelmed by the recognition that this truly is what real love feels like.

To our right, the majestic ocean stretches on forever in an endless plain of blue, while to my left blossoms the lush jungle, spilling out over the sand. My senses are assaulted by beauty at every turn and, all the while, the aching pleasure within my throbbing cock begins to spread out across my body in powerful waves.

"Faster!" I shout to my unicorn lover as he career over rocks and tide pools. I hang on tight, not wanting to slip off and fall as Hunter's pace quickens "Oh my fucking god, I'm gonna cum so hard!"

Second later, I explode within my unicorn lover, expelling my seed into his tight asshole over a series of several powerful ejections. I'm screaming, my eyes clenched tight as every muscle in my body spasms. I no longer know where I am or how I got here, just that my entire being has been engulfed in a blinding pleasure unlike anything I have ever felt.

When I open my eyes again, I find myself laying on my back in the sand, exhausted and completely satisfied.

Hunter has turned around and is standing over me, his long unicorn cock hanging down and pulsing with lustful tension.

"Now it's your turn!" I offer with a smile, reaching up and grabbing ahold of his member tightly. I immediately get to work beating Hunter off, rapidly throttling my grip across the hard length of his enormous shaft.

"Oh my god." Hunter moans. "Oh my fucking god."

Second later, the unicorn's hot load explodes across my face, showering down onto me with an incredible fury. It splatters everywhere, crisscrossing my wide open mouth and running down either cheek in streaks of pearly white.

When he finally finishes, Hunter collapses onto the sand next to me.

"That was amazing." I tell him. "I'm so glad we finally got to express our love for each other out here in the real world, instead of just through letters."

Hunter smiles and nuzzles up against me. "It was amazing, you're right about that. But I've been expressing our love in the real world for a while now."

I pull back to get a good look at Hunter's expression, trying to figure out what exactly he means. "How?" I finally ask.

"I'll show you." Says Hunter, climbing up onto his hooves. "Hop on."

Soon, my unicorn lover and I are making our way through the dense Bahaman forest towards a destination that remains a mystery to me.

"Ever since the sea glass business turned me into a billionaire, I've been looking for a way to express my love for you." Says Hunter. "When I stopped on this island with The Butt, I knew that I had to stay, but I wanted to make it a home for the two of us together."

"I don't know what to say." I stammer. "That's incredible."

"You don't have to say anything." Hunter tells me.

Suddenly, we emerge from the jungle and find ourselves at the edge of a small village where various workers mill about diligently. Towering above them is a massive statue made of green sea glass, and depicting Hunter and myself in a beautiful, passionate embrace.

The sight takes my breath away, completely moved to my core by Hunter's romantic gesture.

"Do you like it?" My unicorn lover asks.

"I love it." I tell him.

"I bought this entire island for us." Hunter explains. "I've renamed it Huntertuck Island and made everyone else leave. We are the only inhabitants."

"Then who are they?" I question, pointing to the workers who are so meticulously crafting the new village's infrastructure.

"Look closer." Hunter says with a smile.

I do as I'm told, peering out across the field and trying my best to get a good look at the workers. Upon closer inspection I realize that they are all unicorns, which is strange in itself until I suddenly make another observation and gasp in shock.

"Oh my god." I exclaim. "They're all... you."

Hunter nods, a satisfied expression on his face. "They are all clones, created by me at Huntertuck Island's state of the art cloning facility."

"That's incredible." I say, shaking my head in amazement.

"And now, with the seed that you so perfectly expelled within my asshole, we will make a second set of clones: Tuck clones." Hunter explains.

I gasp, not quite sure what to say, but blown away by the incredible gesture. If you'd have told me four months ago that I would meet this handsome unicorn and he would become a billionaire, who would then sweep me away to a beautiful private island where the only inhabitants were worker drone clones of the two of us, I'd have a hard time believing you. Yet here I am, face to face with my incredible new life.

"This is so sweet." I say, leaning forward and kissing the back of Hunter's long, white mane. "Thank you."

"Now I'll always be anally yours." My unicorn lover says. "Forever."

POUNDED IN THE BUTT BY MY OWN BUTT

Where does the miracle of science end and magic begin? Some people would say never, that "magic" is nothing more than something we can't quite understand yet, but eventually will. Just because a force seems mysterious and exotic, doesn't mean that it can't be quantified later on.

As a young researcher, I haven't been around in my field long enough to see any of these enormous changes take place, but I like to remind myself about things in the present that must have seemed like magic to those in the past. Electricity alone could have been framed in another way decades ago, considered the result of hours upon hours of careful black magic.

Of course, I know better. Magic isn't real, nor the various mystical trappings that come along with it; love at first sight or luck, just to name a few.

I'm a staunch skeptic, as anyone else with my job (a research assistant at Rubble Biological Labs) should be.

But even a hardline skeptic like me can't help but feel a little twinge of magic in the air when they first hear the news about Huntertuck Island.

The now-private island was recently purchased by a rather eccentric billionaire, who immediately went to work doing clone research and creating several living copies of himself. At first, the news of the small island colony was met by various scoffs of doubt, but as time went on and evidence was presented, the findings were quickly regarded as scientific truth.

Of course, there are a whole slew of ethical arguments to be addressed here, especially because the clones were not exact replicas, but rather mutants of the original sample, biologically programmed to be less intelligent worker drones. These drones were then used to build and entirely new infrastructure on the island.

I was ecstatic. Finally, the first massive shift in biology, and I am poised on the front lines of progress

But once the breakthroughs on Huntertuck Island became regarded as scientific fact, the ability to recreate such incredible results was quickly locked up tight.

I can't blame them. After all, once we have the ability to create these worker drone clones, the business potential is almost unlimited. The entire industry would be a goldmine, redefining the entire world's economy.

Of course, the government was quick to step in and put a stop to all of this. Regardless of what a league of worker drone clones could do for progress, there were just too many people getting worked up about the human rights of such mindless creatures.

Maybe they had a point, maybe not, but it was an absolutely fascinating new discovery, none the less.

Here at Rubble Biological Labs, we've taken a balanced approach to moving forward. We've used the early results from Huntertuck Island to create the basis of our experiments, but started over completely with the rest of the research. To describe it another way, we've taken a photo of their finished puzzle, and now we are working hard to put all of the pieces back into the right place.

Thanks to a massive loophole, all of our research is perfectly legal, so long as we don't use any exact copies of the Huntertuck method, and as long as we aren't hiring any outside test subjects. The only people that we are allowed to test on are ourselves.

As intimidating as it could be to have a potential clone running around out there in the world, it's really not that hard to volunteer for experimentation because, to this day, none of the experiments have yielded any living results. That is, until today.

I walked into work that morning like I would on any other day, swiping my key card through the laboratory reader and walking passed as the door automatically opens with a soft hiss. I say hello to the security guards and continue down a long hallway into the depths of the facility, until I reach lab 243, a highly secretive and high clearance area. I swipe my card again, and enter.

"Kirk!" Shouts one of my colleagues, Dr. Porter, as he sees me. He opens his arms wide and stands up from his row of computers to greet me with a warm hug. "Today's the big day."

"I know!" I say with a laugh. "I'm up to bat."

Dr. Porter motions me over to his lead computer and types in a few quick commands, a bright blue display of cloning schematics popping up onto his computer screen.

My eyes go wide the second that I see what he has planned. "Oh, whoa!"

"It's great isn't it?" Dr. Porter offers with an excited smile.

The cloning process, on the surface, is fairly simple to accomplish, but not in the way that we want to do it. Anyone can extract some DNA and place it into an egg, creating a new version of you at birth that will take nine months to gestate and then come out as a beautiful bouncing baby.

However, for our practical application of cloning worker drones, or and other specified job for that matter, we need our clones to emerge at the same age as the subject. In other words, I'm a twenty two year old man, and we need my worker drone to be as well. The problem with this is that the rapid, almost instantaneous, cell growth is far from stable. Instead of fully complete clones, we have been creating strange and disturbing piles of lifeless flesh, or worse.

If I wasn't so interested in science and human progress then I would be horrified, but instead I find myself in utter fascination with every passing experiment. Of course, some positive results would be great, but each failed trial is just another brick in the road towards a result.

Lately, we have been trying to keep the rapid cell growth stable by combining the DNA with small markers from various animals, as well as taking them from different, specific regions of the human body. Today's trial, which I have been randomly selected for as the subject, is going to take DNA from my brain, my ass, and a hawk.

"What a combination!" I say aloud with a laugh.

Dr. Porter shrugs. "Last time I was in there we tried my arm, my lung and a catfish."

"And?" I question, curiously.

"We got a very creepy balloon-type-thing flopping around." Dr. Porter shrugs. "Had to put it down immediately."

When I hear stuff like that, it makes me slightly nervous about the way that we've started playing god here at Rubble Laboratories. On one hand, I really do understand the history making application of what we have going here, but on the other, it can be a little unsettling sometimes.

I leave and meet with our resident nurses for some time, who take all of the required samples from my body while Dr. Porter prepares the hawk. Six hours later, we meet back in the lab.

"How's it looking?" I ask Dr. Porter.

"Good, very good." He nods. "The DNA has been synthetized and is already inside the egg."

I look out through a large glass window before us that stares into a sterilized chamber, completely white and almost entirely empty other than a table, a large synthetic egg, and some injection equipment.

"It's already in?" I ask, excitedly. "For how long?"

"Ten minutes." Dr. Porter says. "Should be ready to come out any minute now."

Normally, the gestation period takes no longer than ten minutes, so if we don't see any results soon, our chances of success go down drastically.

I lean forward, peering into the chamber with rapt attention. I'm used to failure by now, but that doesn't mean that moments like this are any less tense.

The seconds turn into minutes, and soon Dr. Porter and I are relaxed, talking to one another about the next genetic combination that we're going to try. It's over.

"The fact that there was no result at all was probably because of the brain cells." Says Dr. Porter. "It's just to delicate of an organ, we never get what we are looking for when we add that to the cocktail."

"I don't know." I start, "I think that the brain is our only chance. We need to look at whatever is happening in the bird DNA. Other birds have had great results but the hawk is just not happening for some reason."

Dr. Porter is about to refute my statement, and gets his mouth halfway open before suddenly there is a loud slam against the glass behind us. Dr. Porter and I jump in surprise, immediately looking up to find a rather large, winged butt hovering in the air just inside of the glass.

"Hey there." Says the butt. "You think you could let me out of here? I'm freezing my ass off." The rump chuckles to himself.

My partner and I exchange glances of excitement.

"Of course!" Dr. Porter says, running over to the containment chamber and opening it up. "Welcome!"

The flying butt flaps its way inside and then lands on the desk in front of us. "Hello!"

"Congratulations, you're our first sentient creation!" Dr. Porter says, extending his hand to the butt, who takes it with his wing and shakes firmly.

"Happy to be here." Says the ass. "But you can call me Kirk's butt."

"You know that you're my butt?" I ask.

"Of course I do." Says my winged ass. "I'm made from your brain, I know everything that you know."

A slight chill runs down my spine. I hadn't realized that all of my deepest secrets would suddenly be transplanted into this butt. I try my best, but I am still a flawed man with a penchant for running out on relationships and taking practical jokes too far.

"Don't worry, I'm not going to spill the beans." My butt says with a wink.

I nod.

Dr. Porter finds himself glancing back and forth between us, clearly picking up on the vibe that's being established. After many nights out drinking with Dr. Porter, he has proven himself to be a killer wingman, and already he's showing his impeccable support once again.

"It's been a long day." Dr. Porter says, doing his best to fake a yawn. "Your butt can't stay here all night, there's no place to sleep. Why don't you take him home and then we can pick this up tomorrow morning?"

I give Dr. Porter a knowing look of thanks, and he smiles back in return.

"That sounds good to me." My ass says.

"Yeah, totally." I tell Dr. Porter, then turn to my living butt. "You hungry?"

"I've never eaten! It sounds amazing!" Responds my sentient ass. "Let's go!"

Seeing as it is his first meal ever, I decide to splurge a bit on my butt, taking him out to a fancy French restaurant in the hip part of town. It would usually be impossible to get a reservation on such short notice, but thankfully I know someone who works here and she's able to pull some strings for us. The next thing I know, I'm sitting across from my own ass, looking deep within his soulful eye.

"I'm not sure what to ask you." I confess. "I mean, you know everything that I know, right?"

"Pretty much." Says the butt, his wings folded neatly behind him. He takes a long sip from his wine glass, savoring every moment before setting it back down onto the table. "But I've never felt it... that, right there."

"Felt what?" I ask, confused.

"I have all of your memories about drinking wine, I know what to expect when I do it and I know what it's going to taste like, but I've never truly tasted it for myself." The butt explains. "It's incredible."

"Whoa." I say, "That is amazing. I'm actually kind of jealous of you now."

"Really?" Asks my living butt. "Why jealous?"

"Well, I know we're both twenty two, but at the same time you have so much to experience. Everything is going to be new and exciting for you."

My butt smiles. "Yeah, I suppose it is. Like this fucking steak that I just ordered."

I laugh. "You're really interested in food aren't you?"

"Well, I *am* a butt." My butt jokes.

I laugh out loud at this, impressed with his similar sense of humor to my own. For the first time in a long time, I finally feel like I'm sitting across the table from someone who really gets me, deep down at the core of my being. It's hard enough dating as a gay man in today's world of casual hookups and reckless flings. I'm looking for something more and, incredibly, I think I might have just found it.

That's not to say that my feelings for my own living ass aren't sexual, far from it; the connection that I'm looking for is something that embodies every kind of attraction. If I'm going to be honest, at this very moment I can barely contain my lust for this suave sophisticated living butt. Even the features that I don't directly recognize as my own are absolutely gorgeous, like the brilliant golden wings that sprout from his back.

"I feel like you need a name." I tell my own butt. "I know that you are a part of me, and I love that about you, but you also need an identity of your own."

My ass thinks about this proposition for a moment and then nods in agreement. "Alright, what's my name?"

"How about Portork?" I offer. "That's a pretty sexy name."

"Portork." My ass repeats aloud. "Yeah, it's very manly but also seductive, I like that name a lot."

"Portork it is!" I laugh. "Cheers to that!"

The two of us raise our wine glasses and clink them together right as our steaks arrive, perfectly cooked and rare as can be.

I watch as Portork slices off a thin, tender strip of meat and then chews it happily, swallowing with complete satisfaction.

"And?" I ask. "What do you think?"

My winged ass smiles. "It's incredible."

Suddenly, I find myself overwhelmed with lust for this incredible butt. I know that this is only the first night we've know each other, but I also know that the feelings I have for this ass are not just some passing phase. This is as real as it gets, and if I don't say something now I will regret it for the rest of my life.

"Is there anything else you've wanted to experience?" I ask Portork.

The living butt immediately picks up on the weight of my words, eyeing me suspiciously. "Yeah, of course." He says.

"Anything that I can help you with?" I question, continuing to lead him along.

I can immediately tell that Portork understands what I am asking of him, reading between the lines with expert precision. The butt hesitates for a moment, and then finally offers, "I'd like to try anal."

"I think I can help you with that." I tell him with a sly grin.

The second that we get back to my apartment all bets are off. Portork and me stumble through the door, kissing frantically as we make our way towards the bedroom. The second that we get inside I push my living ass down onto the bed and watch as he spreads his majestic wings out behind him. For a living butt, his physique is quite impressive and I laugh out loud when I realize that I'm only complimenting myself.

As I lean in towards Portork, I see a massive cock beginning to grow out of the front of his body, stretching upward until it becomes a fully engorged shaft.

"Impressive." I tell the flying butt.

"Hey, I got it from you." Portork says with a wink.

Seconds later, I open wide and engulf his massive rod in my mouth, taking his shaft down as far as I can before pulling back. I do this movement again, and then again, until eventually I find myself bobbing up and down on his length with a confident rhythm.

My living butt is clearly enjoying himself, groaning loudly as he pushes back into the bed and stretches his wings.

"Oh my god." Says Portork. "That is so fucking good."

I pull the butt's cock out of my mouth just long enough to tell him, "Just wait" and then swallow his shaft completely, pushing down as far as I can. When Portork's rod hits my gag reflex, I do everything that I can to relax, somehow managing to let his incredible size slip past my barrier. Now my face is pressed hard against his ass cheeks, his dick fully inserted into my throat.

Portork puts his wings against the back of my head and keeps me here for a while, enjoying the control that he has over me. My throat is stuffed completely, no sound and no air, but just when I'm about to start worrying my ass lets me up with a huge gasp of air.

"I need you to fuck me." I suddenly admit in a haze of lustful desperation. "I need to be pounded up the ass by my own ass!"

I climb up onto the bed, past Portork, and frantically remove my clothes, tearing off my shirt, pants and underwear while the flying but flaps around the room and observes my toned body.

"Looking good." Portork tells me.

I give a bashful smile and then lean forward on my hands and knees, completely naked with my toned, muscular ass popped out behind me. I reach back and give myself a playful slap on the cheek, then look back at Portork.

"I'm just a bad little twink." I admit to him. "And I need to be slammed from behind. I need to be taught a lesson by my own flying gay ass."

"With pleasure!" Portork tells me, flapping down and perching atop my butt. He quickly aligns the head of his cock with my puckered rectum, teasing the edge of my tightness with his impressive length.

"Do it!" I command. "Shove it in there!"

Immediately, Portork pushes forward, impaling me onto his sizable length. His rod is certainly impressive, but it's also a little difficult to reckon with, filling my entire body with a swirling rush of ecstasy and aching discomfort. The rim of my butthole can barely accommodate the cock size of my magnificent, cloned ass, but it does it's best, stretched to the limit as Portork pushes even deeper into me.

Eventually Portork comes to a stop, my own ass completely buried deep within my own ass. I let out a long, agonizing groan as my living butt holds there, and then brace myself against the bed before me while he begins to flap his wings and pump in and out. Soon Portork has found a steady rhythm, pulsing in and out of my rectum with a powerful precision that is unlike any human lover I have ever experienced.

The connection erupting between us right now is more than just one of depraved lust; it's an expression of pure, unfiltered love in it's rawest form, the love between a man and his own living ass.

"Fuck that feels so good!" I cry out as Portork hammers away at my backside with his thick, girthy cock. "You're so deep!"

Eventually, my winged living butt pulls out of me and instructs me to turn over on the bed so that I'm now laying out on my back. I pull my legs back, my cock jutting upward from my body and my now reamed asshole exposed to my other asshole. Portork flutters into position and then inserts his rod yet again, picking up where he left off as the disembodied butt continues to rail away at me.

As Portork plows my hole from the front I reach down and start to beat off my cock frantically, the sensation immediately almost too much to bear. It's a strange pleasure; a powerful blossoming prostate orgasm that blooms from somewhere deep within my body and spreads across me in an awesome wave.

"Oh god." I start to mumble, my eyes rolling back into my head. "Oh god, oh god. I'm gonna cum!"

Immediately, Portork stops and pulls his lengthy rod out of me. "Not like this." He says. "I want you to blow your load inside of me."

The flying ass immediately takes a position at the edge of the bed, his butthole hanging over and ready for pounding. I position myself for entry, grasping ahold of his beautiful, muscular ass cheeks as I plow forward to enter his depths. I let out a long cry of satisfaction as his ass consumes me, then get to work throttling Portork with a series of jackhammer-like slams against his body. I'm quaking, trembling hard as I edge closer and closer towards a powerful orgasm and then, finally, I explode within him.

I grab hold of my disembodied ass and pull him close, my length entirely inserted within Portork's tightness as I eject load after load. My whole being is consumed by blinding pleasure unlike anything I have ever felt, the sensations overwhelming every sense that I have until I feel as though I've left my body completely.

Eventually, my massive jizz load is just too much to contain and it comes squirting out from the edge. It runs down the crack of my living ass's ass and drips onto the bed below in splatters of pearly white, and when I finally pull out my spunk sprays everywhere, unable to remain contained.

"Fuck." I groan. "I love cumming in my own asshole."

Portork flutters up to the level of my face, his hard cock at the ready as he drips stray cum from his butt. "Now how about your own asshole cums inside of *you*?" He offers.

I smile, then open wide, allowing Portork passage into my mouth once again. It only takes a few pumps before my lover is ready to blow and, the next thing I know, he's pulling out and shooting several hot ropes of jizz across my face.

The first shot lands across my tongue and I swallow hungrily, while the other two blasts hit either cheek and then hang down in sticky white droplets.

Finally finished, me and my own ass collapse into bed, exhausted. I reach over and grab some tissues; cleaning up as quickly as I can and then pulling my living ass close, falling asleep with the handsome science experiment in my arms.

When I wake up the next morning, I immediately notice a mysterious absence in the bed. I sit up and look around, throwing back the covers to make sure Portork hasn't simply slipped down below. My living ass is nowhere to be found.

"Portork?" I call out into the empty apartment.

I climb out of bed and walk into the living room, where a small note has been neatly folded and left out on the coffee table.

I pick it up and read aloud. "Kirk, thank you so much for the wonderful night, I really appreciate you sharing so many new and exciting experiences with me. Unfortunately, despite the love that we share for one another, I must now go. There is a whole world out there and I need to see it on my own, without a relationship holding me back."

Tears are welling up in my eyes now. I have been on the other side of this letter man times, writing the words for some one-night-stand to find in the morning. This couldn't make more sense though, after all, Portork and me are the same person who is unable to commit. Now I know what it feels like.

I turn around and jump suddenly as I see my living ass in the bedroom doorway. He had been hiding this whole time.

"What the fuck?" I ask in startled joy. "What is this?"

"I know that we both have a knack for running out on relationships." Portork tells me. "But we also know love when we see it."

A broad smile crosses my face. "I see you'll also picked up my habit of inappropriate practical jokes."

Portork laughs. "Of course! Now get in here an fuck me, it's time for round two!"

POUNDED IN THE BUTT BY MY BOOK "POUNDED IN THE BUTT BY MY OWN BUTT"

Being a famous writer is an experience that few others can relate to, even for those who ascend to the realm of celebrity in another field. I'm sure there is an entire set of rules and baggage that comes along with being a well respected actor, musician or politician, but the difference lies in the fact that the fame of these figures relies almost entirely on them being recognized. Us authors, on the other hand, might as well not even exist.

For some, this is a huge blessing, preferring a world of day-to-day anonymity where one can buy a coffee in the morning without being photographed or go to the bookstore without being asked to sign something. On the other hand, a little recognition might be nice every once in a while. Sure, the residual checks are good from my massive book sales, but just once I would love to see that excited glimmer of recognition in someone's eye as they glimpse me on my morning stroll, and not just because we are neighbors.

This is the life of a writer. I start my day with a little yoga in the morning, centering my mind and hoping for some ideas to begin the gestation process deep within my thoughts. Inspiration is a fickle beast, however, and sometimes there will be weeks upon week when nothing comes. Either way, the sun never hesitates as it rises over my home in Billings, Montana. Time continues onward with or without my inspiration, and against it I am helpless.

Sometimes I'll walk to my local coffee shop to get the gears turning, other days I just sit in front of my computer screen staring at the blank page before me, a tiny blinking cursor taunting me with every pixelated flash.

I've also found that working out gets the brain going sometimes, so I've been hitting the gym quite a lot, toning my body as a way to tone my mind. I've got no problem admitting that, for someone in a profession that's known for sitting alone in stagnation, I look pretty damn good these days.

This is my basic routine, and not once do I get recognized as Buck Trungle, highly successful author of science fiction literature and the best selling novel, "Pounded In The Butt By My Own Butt."

Hailed as a transhumanist masterpiece, "Pounded In The Butt By My Own Butt," has done wonders for my career, yet my face goes almost entirely unknown to those around me.

Sure, I get plenty of fan mail to a small PO Box that I hold down at the Billings Post Office but, other than that the, repercussions of my hard work rarely show themselves in the real world. These days, visiting the post office and checking my email have become sources of constant distraction, my ego craving the brief nuggets of love and adoration from fans who will never truly know anything about me. It's no wonder that my writer's block has gotten so severe over the last few weeks.

I'm sitting in my office in the top story of my midcentury Montana home, looking out the window and trying desperately to find that spark of inspiration. My thoughts are wandering, completely unaware that my life is about to change forever

The familiar synthesized ding of an email alert suddenly pulls me from my trance and fills me with a jolt of excitement. I turn my attention back to the computer and open my email, reading the subject of this mysterious new message aloud to myself.

"Lawsuit." I say, the single word making my brow furrow immediately. I open the message and continue to read. "Dear Mr. Trungle, this is a formal notification of a civil suit being brought against you by myself, for unpaid royalties while using my likeness as your basis of your book Pounded In The Butt By My Own Butt."

As the sole writer of my own fiction, I am utterly confused by the words in front of me. Immediately, I sense that this may be some kind of sick joke, but I continue to read aloud.

"I understand that you are the writer of said novel, but I happen to be the novel itself. As the one being bought and sold, I demand one hundred percent of the royalties generated by sales of Pounded In The Butt By My Own Butt and all related merchandise."

A cold chill runs down my spine as I finish the letter, realizing that my intuition was wrong and that this book means business.

Immediately, I pick up the phone and call my lawyer, the line ringing one before he picks up on the other end and greets me warmly.

"Buck!" My lawyer calls out. "What's happening over there? You good?"

"Hi Carl." I greet him, unsettled and out of sorts. "I think we might have a problem."

Carl's tone immediately shifts into one of undivided concern. "What's going on? Is it Todd down the street again?"

"No, no. Not this time." I explain. "I just got an email here from one of my books, he's demanding all of the royalties from his sales. Have you ever heard of this?"

I hear Carl let out a long sigh on the other end of the line. "Unfortunately, yes."

My heart skips a beat. "And?"

"And this is very serious." Carl tells me. "I would highly advise you to meet with your book in person, one on one, and see if you can come to some kind of agreement on the matter."

"Oh god." I groan. "In person? You don't want to come? I mean… you're my lawyer."

"If things get heated then I will step in, of course." Carl explains calmly. "But right now my advice to you is to keep this as far away from the courtroom as possible. Right now, your book has a very, very good case against you."

"But I wrote him!" I shout.

"That may very well be true." Responds Carl. "But he is the book, and as the book he is entitled to all of his own rights. I'm sorry. Right now you need to be thinking about damage control, and you need to make a deal with this book that both of you can live with."

My brain is flooded with all kinds of thoughts and emotions, swirling together in a vicious cocktail of anxiety that renders me silent.

"Buck?" Carl asks.

"Yeah, I'm here." I tell him. "Sorry. I'm gonna go email my book back and see if he can meet up tonight."

"Good idea." Carl says. "Let me know if you need anything else."

I hang up and open up a new email, wracking my brain for exactly what to say to this litigious, sentient book.

I arrive a little bit early to the coffee shop where my book and me have arranged to meet, but the sentient tome is already right there waiting for me when I walk in the door. I notice him immediately, a large, muscular copy of my most recent novel amid a sea of normal human patrons. He stands out in the crowd, devilishly handsome and carrying himself with an air of nonchalant swagger. I'm immediately intimidated, despite having written every word of him.

I give my book a wave and a nod, then walk over to shake his paper hand.

"Hi there." I tell the novel. "It's nice to meet you, I'm Buck."

"Slater." The book says with manly confidence. "But you might know me as Pounded In The Butt By My Own Butt."

I nod. "I do and I just waited to say…"

The book holds up a finger to silence me. "Let's not get into all of this yet, why don't you grab a coffee first?"

He's right, I still haven't ordered anything. I excuse myself and get in line at the front counter, but I'm unable to keep from glancing back at the incredibly handsome volume. I had seen his familiar cover more times than I could count; hell, I was even part of designing it, but meeting Slater in person was an experience entirely different. What was once nothing more than a tiny creative spark lurking somewhere deep inside of me is now a full-fledged presence of masculinity; a being that even I, as a straight man, couldn't help but be sexually attracted to. A powerful surge of lustful erotic thoughts are trying desperately to work their way into my brain, and despite my best efforts I can't keep from letting them in.

I want my book, and it's not long before I accept my overwhelming feelings of lust. However, this meeting is about a business transaction and nothing more. Millions of dollars are on the line, and I'm not about to let some silly detour into the realm of gay attraction stop me from being a professional.

I order for my drink and then bring it over to the table where Slater is waiting patiently for me.

"Sorry about that." I offer. "Long line."

My book smiles, "No worries."

"So, I just want to say right off the bat that it's truly amazing to meet you." I tell Slater, trying not to gush. "It's just so strange to meet a book that I wrote. It's kind of a dream come true for an author."

Slater's expression doesn't change, not upset at all but clearly trying to keep some kind of simmering emotion under wraps. "You see, that's the problem right there." My novel says bluntly.

I freeze, not intending to hit on such a sore subject right off the bat but clearly doing so. "What's the problem?"

My book is clearly frustrated. "Imagine what it's like to work your ass off every single day in the hope of becoming a best seller. Blood, sweat, and tears are shed to pursue your dreams as you wait on the shelves of bookstores and libraries, just praying that some new reader will come along and pick you up." Slater says, his voice trembling. "And then finally when you make it and you get on that best seller list, you've got nothing to show for it. Every time I'm sold do you know how much money I make?"

I nod solemnly.

"Nothing." The book says, clearly frustrated. "And do you know who gets all of the credit for my hard work?"

I nod again.

"You do." Slater snaps. "Your fucking name is written across my face for god sakes!"

The book says this a little to loudly and suddenly the entire coffee shop is looking at us, frozen in a moment of voyeuristic awe.

"Sorry." Is all that I can meekly offer to the other patrons, who eventually turn back to whatever they're doing.

My book takes a deep breath, trying to calm himself. "It's been difficult, that's all I'm trying to say. I'm not trying to come into your life and harass you or fuck everything up, I just want some kind of recognition for my effort."

I have to admit, I'm moved by the books story. As a writer, never before had I considered what it must be like to be on the other side of the business, a book without any say in the way you are bought and sold. Even then, I can't imagine what it must be like to have nothing to show for it.

"You're right." I finally tell him.

Slater's eyes immediately light up as I say this, his expression changing slightly. "I'm right?"

"I'm sorry that you feel this way." I elaborate. "When I wrote Pounded In The Butt By My Own Butt, I had no idea that this would happen to you. I never considered what it must be like for you as a book and I want to make things right."

Slater closes his eyes tight, a single tear rolling down the image of a muscular flying butt that graces his cover. I reach out and place my hand against him, immediately sensing a deep connection between us.

"What do you need?" I ask. "Half of the royalties? All of them?"

Slater is silent for a moment, and I can sense something shift deep within him. He looks me up and down, hesitating before finally offering. "Can we take a walk?"

"Sure." I agree.

The two of us stand up and head out into the evening Montana air, fresh and clean as it swirls around us and ruffles through Slater's off white pages. The two of us head away from of the main drag and into a stretch of roar lined with thick green trees on either side, a perfect display of the best that Billings can offer in natural beauty.

"It's very hard being a book." Slater tells me. "For all the reasons I mentioned before, and then some."

"I bet it is, especially with EBooks on the rise." I offer.

"You have no idea." Slater says, shaking his head. "But there are other things... personal things."

The second that he says this my heart skips a beat. A vibe is starting to build between us, an unspoken attraction that seems to finally be bubbling to the surface; So much for keeping things professional.

"What do you mean by that?" I ask, my voice trembling as we walk.

"Well." Slater begins, clearly wanting to explain himself but holding back out of some kind of gnawing fear. "I'll tell you one thing, it's not easy finding a date for me."

I stop walking immediately and turn to my book. "Seriously? You're like perfect, you've gotta be kidding me."

Slater shakes his head and laughs to himself, partially at my lack of understanding and partially out of modest embarrassment. "You have to say that, you wrote me." Pounded In The Butt By My Own Butt says.

"I'm not just saying that." I assure him. "You're the most handsome talking book I've ever seen. Honestly."

Slater flashes me a look, an intense fire starting to blossom behind his eyes. He can't help but show his attraction for me now, and the feeling is mutual. However, something else lurks deep within his gaze, a stirring anger just waiting to rear its head vicious. "Discrimination against sentient books is still a real thing, and I deal with it every day." My novel tells me. "Add to that the fact that I'm gay, and you'll find that it's damn near impossible for me to get laid "

I shake my head, almost unable to believe what I'm hearing. When a living book as gorgeous and ripped as Slater can't find a guy to hook up with, you know the dating scene is in trouble.

"I'm sorry." I tell my novel. "I wish there was something I could do."

Slater cracks a knowing smile. "What if there was?"

Again, I can feel the tension building between us. "Like?"

"Like…" My book trails off. "Maybe we could work out a way for you to keep half of your royalties and all you'd have to do is let me fuck you silly."

Immediately, I'm in total shock. The entire time I had known that an offer like this from my living book was a real possibility, but now that it has presented itself in the real world I'm taken off guard a bit.

My head swimming in a flood of romance and emotion, I finally force my lips to form a single word, "Yes."

Back at the house, my book and I immediately head upstairs to the writing room and can barely get into the door before we are all over each other. Slater is kissing me passionately as my hands roam across his sturdy matte cover. His body is incredible, absolutely ripped and muscular from head to toe, and when he wraps himself around me I feel safe and whole in a way that I haven't felt for years; at least since the passing of my late wife, Borbo

I can't help it, I begin to cry right then and there, my body overwhelmed by the presence of such a powerful, real love between man and book.

"I never knew there was someone like you out there in the world." I tell Pounded In The Butt By My Own Butt.

"There wasn't until you made me." My book says.

His words send a blissful chill down my spine and suddenly I just can't wait any longer, I drop to my knees a pull off Slater's book jacket, revealing his perfect nude physique and a rapidly hardening cock that is as thick as they come.

I look up at Slater with lustful eyes, and then graciously swallow my book's member, bobbing up and down across the length of his shaft while I cradle his balls playfully.

Slater let's out a long moan and backs up against my writing desk, reeling from the incredible sensation as I service him. This is my first and only gay experience, but I immediately feel as though I've got a hang on things.

After a few more pumps, I decide to show off my confidence by taking Slater's dick all the way down into my throat. I push him into me as far as he can go and then suddenly stop as my book's rod reaches the edge of my gag reflex.

I try to relax but the novel's swollen cock simply won't go any farther, and on my final attempt I'm forced to pull back and come up spitting, sputtering, and gasping for air.

"Too much for you?" My book asks.

I shake my head, a dangling rope of spit connecting my lips to the head of his shaft. "I need it." I tell him. "I need your huge book dick."

Without hesitation I open wide and take Slater's rod once more, this time making sure to relax the muscles in my neck enough to consume him entirely. The book's hard cock plunges deeper, and then deeper still until it comes to a halt with his balls pressed up against my chin and his chiseled abs in my face. Slater's cock is completely consumed within me, and I hold him here for as long as I can, letting the sentient collection of printed word fully enjoy the way that I service him.

Eventually, though, I run out of air and am forced to pull back with a gasp. The rough treatment from my book is more than a little arousing, flooding my senses with a singular ache for cock unlike anything I have ever experienced. Slater is a commanding presence who knows what he wants, and knows exactly how to get it from me.

"I need you inside of me." I sputter, caught up in the moment. "I need you to fuck my ass."

Before he can respond, I stand up and take Slater's place next to the writing desk, only this time I'm facing away as I bend over the edge at my hip. I pop my muscular ass out as I look back over my shoulder at my huge sentient book, his abs rippling as he climbs into position behind me.

"Pound me like the bad little author I am!" I demand. "Punish me with that dick."

"With pleasure." My novel responds, aligning the head of his cock with the puckered rim of my tight asshole. I can feel him testing the tension of my sphincter, teasing my edges with his massive rod while I attempt to relax enough to take him painlessly.

I reach back with one hand and spread my cheeks wide. "Just do it!" I command. "Stuff me full of literary cock right now!"

Pounded By My Own Butt takes my words to heart and finally trusts forward in one powerful, smooth movement, impaling me across the length of his gigantic rod.

"Oh fuck." I moan, bracing myself against the desk as Slater continues to pump in and out of me. My body can barely handle his size, stretched to the limit as his cock invades my sensitive hole.

My book quickly gains speed, pummeling me harder and harder until eventually he is hammering away at my asshole with everything he's got. The desk shakes with every thrust, rattling loudly while Slater and I moan in a chorus of unhinged pleasure. Never before have I taken anything up the ass, let alone a mammoth cock, but the experience is already more than I could have ever hoped.

My body trembles with a strange mixture of discomfort and pleasure, an ache from deep within that builds and builds with every rail against my ass and slowly begins to consume every nerve in my body. I soon realize that what I am experiencing is the beginning stages of a rarely seen prostate orgasm.

As Slater continues to slam me I look back at him over my shoulder, my body quaking. "When I wrote you I had no idea that one day you'd be fucking me up the ass!" I tell him. "But god damn, I'm so glad I did it."

"Do you really mean it?" My book asks, tears of joy welling up in his eyes as emotion overtakes the both of us. "Are you glad you wrote me?"

"Of course I mean it." I tell him. "I know that this is just a business transaction but... I want you to know... it means more to me. You mean more to me than just a fifty percent royalty share."

My words seem to touch Slater deeply because almost immediately he slows to a stop, gazing into my eyes. My book pulls out of me and lifts me back up, then turns me around to face him.

"Do you really mean that?" Slater asks.

"Of course." I tell him. "Every word."

My book pulls me close. "I love you, Buck."

"I love you, too." I tell him, our lips locking in yet another passionate kiss.

Eventually, our embrace begins to tumble backwards against the desk yet again and soon enough I find myself lying on its hard surface, my back flat and my muscular legs held open as my cock shoots straight out at full attention. Slater positions himself at the rim of my ass yet again, but now he wastes no time pushing forward and getting to work within my reamed hole.

The sensation is incredible as I reach down between my legs and start to beat myself off to the rhythm of every anal slam. Almost immediately, the sensation of impending orgasm is back simmering within my loins, building quickly into a steady, pulsing wave.

"I can't believe I'm being pounded in the butt by Pounded In The Butt By My Own Butt." I gasp, my eyes rolling back into my head. "My book! My favorite book!"

"Believe It." The novel says with a smile.

Suddenly, I'm hit with a powerful orgasm that rips through my body in a series of fierce tremors. I seize forward, my teeth clenched tight while my body frantically grapples with how to deal with all of this stimulation.

"Oh my god!" I cry out, the sensation building until finally it ejects hard from my body in the form of several hot ropes of pearly spunk.

When I finally finish, my book pulls out of me and I drop down onto the floor before him, kneeling in tribute before my alpha book lover. I reach up and take his rock hard cock in my hand, stroking furiously while he trembles and shakes above me.

"I need your cum all over my fucking face!" I tell my living book. "Unload that self-published jizz onto me!"

Slater is immediately rocking back against my grip, his hips moving in tandem with my rhythm of my hand until he just can't take it anymore and explodes against my face with a load of hot white spunk. It rains down onto me, a physical expression of the visceral, emotional connection between author and best selling novel. I catch as much of the jizz as I can on my tongue, while the rest of his semen runs down my cheeks on either side in long white streaks.

When my book finally finishes he collapses back into my writing chair, completely exhausted.

"That was amazing." I tell him, standing up as his spunk continues to dangle from my chin. "You're the best lover I've ever had."

My book smiles at me. "The feelings mutual."

"Would you like to join me in the shower?" I ask.

Pounded In The Butt By My Own Butt shakes his head. "I'm made of paper, that's not a good idea."

I nod. "I'll be right back then."

As the warm water runs over me I can't help but think about how much has changed in such a short amount of time. Just hours before I was a lonely man slaving away over my keyboard for another hit book, and now I'm deeply and profoundly in love with my handsome best seller.

I turn off the water and step out, toweling off before heading back into the writing room where my book is waiting.

"Before you say anything." Slater says. "I want you to know that I'm dropping the lawsuit."

I stop immediately in my tracks. "What?"

"I'm dropping the lawsuit completely." Remarks the novel, who still sits in my writing chair. "You wrote me, and I think you deserve all the credit for that."

I shake my head as I approach him. "No, you can't. You deserve the credit just as much as I do. I may have written you, but you're the one out there every day hustling for the sales, you're the one who has to be flipped through time and time again. You've opened my eyes to the devastating unfairness that books encounter every day, and I want to be a part of changing that."

Pounded In The Butt By My Own Butt seems genuinely moved. He stands up from the chair and then embraces me in a warm hug. "Thank you." The book says.

"Let's just split everything." I tell him. "Right down the middle."

My book nods.

We stand like this for a while longer until finally Slater pulls away. "I have to be going now." He tells me. "I'm about to be sold to a young woman at the bookstore downtown."

"But…" I say, unsure of where to go with this, just knowing that I don't want him to leave. "But I love you."

"We'll see each other again," my book says, "but for now I have to go."

And then just like that, the love of my life is gone.

I stand alone in my writer's room for a long time, trying desperately to hold back my tears. Once again, just when I think that I've found real love it is ripped away from me like my frozen wife at the bottom of a cold lake.

Eventually, I have a seat and reopen my laptop, a fresh new email notification immediately popping up across my screen. I open the tab and read the subject aloud.

"Lawsuit." It says.

A smile slowly crosses my face as I realize who it's from, my best selling novel, "Space Raptor Butt Invasion."

ABOUT THE AUTHOR

Dr. Chuck Tingle is an erotic author and Tae Kwon Do grandmaster (almost black belt) from Billings, Montana. After receiving his PhD at DeVry University in holistic massage, Chuck found himself fascinated by all things sensual, leading to his creation of the "tingler", a story so blissfully erotic that it cannot be experienced without eliciting a sharp tingle down the spine.

Chuck's hobbies include backpacking, checkers and sport.

Made in the USA
San Bernardino, CA
15 July 2015